W9-DJD-310

Dear Dragon Goes to the Zoo

by Margaret Hillert

Illustrated by David Schimmell

NORWOOD HOUSE PRESS

The **Dear Dragon** series is comprised of carefully written books that extend the collection of classic readers you may remember from your own childhood. Each book features text focused on common sight words. Through the use of controlled text, these books provide young children with abundant practice recognizing the words that appear most frequently in written text. Rapid recognition of high-frequency words is one of the keys for developing automaticity which, in turn, promotes accuracy and rate necessary for fluent reading. The many additional details in the pictures enhance the story and offer opportunities for students to expand oral language and develop comprehension.

Shannon Cannon

Shannon K. Cannon, Ph.D.
Literacy Consultant

Norwood House Press • P.O. Box 316598 • Chicago, Illinois 60631
For more information about Norwood House Press please visit our website at
www.norwoodhousepress.com or call 866-565-2900.
Text copyright ©2011 by Margaret Hillert. Illustrations and cover design
copyright ©2011 by Norwood House Press, Inc. All rights reserved. No part of
this book may be reproduced or utilized in any form or by any means without
written permission from the publisher.

This book was manufactured as a paperback edition. If you are purchasing
this book as a rebound hardcover or without any cover, the publisher and any
licensors' rights are being violated.

Paperback ISBN: 978-1-60357-098-5

The Library of Congress has cataloged the original hardcover edition with the
following call number: 2009031727

© 2011 by Norwood House Press. All Rights Reserved. No part of this book may
be reproduced without written permission from the publisher.
This paperback edition was published in 2011.

Printed in Heshan City, Guangdong, China.
187P–082011.

This looks like a good day,
a good day to go somewhere.
Do you want to go to the zoo?

The zoo?
Oh, yes Mother.
That will be fun!

Put this on—
and this—
and get into the car.

Here we go.
Away, away, away.

Here we are at the zoo.
You will like this.

ELEPHANTS→

TIGERS→

GIRAFFES→

←PETTING ZOO

Now we will walk and see things.
Look there!

This is a big one!
And so is the baby.

Oh, oh, oh.
What big cats!
See them run.

Look up there!
Way up, up, UP!

Oh, what a pretty one!
I like that one.

Look here.
The bears have a ball to play with.
A big red ball.

Oh, Father.
Look at this.
It is so big, big, BIG.

Oh, oh, oh.
And look here.
They like to jump!

Mother, look at this brown cow.
It is big.
Big, big, big.

Here is a pretty pony.
It would be fun to ride.

One, two, three.
There are three goats.

And two white bunnies.

This is pretty.
We can eat here.
Come and eat.

This is good, Mother.
This is a good spot.

Here you are with me.
And here I am with you.
What a good, good day, dear dragon.

WORD LIST

Dear Dragon Goes to the Zoo **uses the 78 words listed below.**
This list can be used to practice reading the words that appear in the text.
You may wish to write the words on index cards and use them to help your
child build automatic word recognition. Regular practice with these words
will enhance your child's fluency in reading connected text.

a	Father	now	that
am	fun		the
and		oh	them
are	get	on	there
at	go	one	they
away	goats		things
	good	play	this
baby		pony	three
ball	have	pretty	to
be	here	put	two
bears			
big	I	red	up
brown	into	ride	
bunnies	is	run	walk
	it		want
can		see	way
car	jump	so	we
cats		somewhere	what
come	like	spot	white
cow	look(s)		will
			with
day	me		would
dear	Mother		
do			yes
dragon			you
eat			
			zoo

ABOUT THE AUTHOR

Margaret Hillert has written over 80 books for children who are just learning to read. Her books have been translated into many different languages and over a million children throughout the world have read her books. She first started writing poetry as a child and has continued to write for children and adults throughout her life. A first grade teacher for 34 years, Margaret is now retired from teaching and lives in Michigan where she likes to write, take walks in the morning, and care for her three cats.

ABOUT THE ADVISOR

Shannon K. Cannon is a teacher educator, staff developer, and curriculum writer. She earned her doctorate in Language, Literacy, and Culture from the University of California Davis, where she serves on their clinical faculty supervising pre-service teachers, teaching elementary methods courses in reading/language arts and technology, and teaching Master's courses in inquiry. She began her career teaching second grade. She then spent over 15 years in educational publishing where her work included developing and writing curricular programs as well as providing professional development support to classroom teachers.

ABOUT THE ILLUSTRATOR

David Schimmell served as a professional firefighter for 23 years before hanging up his boots and helmet to devote himself to working as an illustrator of children's books. David has happily created illustrations for the New Dear Dragon books as well as the artwork for educational and retail book projects. Born and raised in Evansville, Indiana, he lives there today with his wife and family.